LIBRARY OF DOOM

THE FINAL CHAPTERS

DON'T OPEN IT!

By Michael Dahl

Illustrated by
Bradford Kendall

Raintree is an imprint of Capstone Global Library Limited, a company
incorporated in England and Wales having its registered office at 7
Pilgrim Street, London, EC4V 6LB – Registered company number: 6695582

www.raintree.co.uk
myorders@raintree.co.uk

Text © Capstone Global Library Limited 2016
The moral rights of the proprietor have been asserted.

Designed by Hilary Wacholz
Original illustrations © Capstone 2016
Illustrated by Bradford Kendall

ISBN 978 1 4747 1054 1 (paperback)
20 19 18 17 16
10 9 8 7 6 5 4 3 2 1

British Library Cataloguing in Publication Data
A full catalogue record for this book is available from
the British Library.

Printed and bound in China.

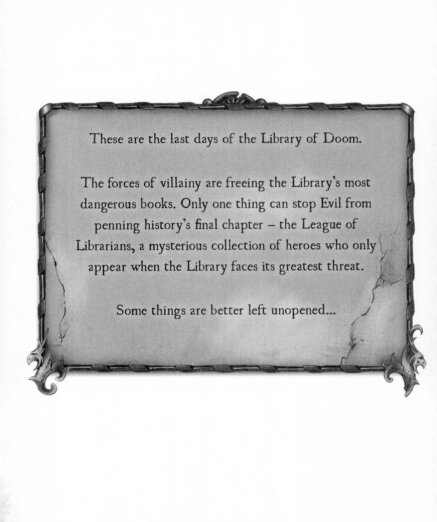

These are the last days of the Library of Doom.

The forces of villainy are freeing the Library's most
dangerous books. Only one thing can stop Evil from
penning history's final chapter – the League of
Librarians, a mysterious collection of heroes who only
appear when the Library faces its greatest threat.

Some things are better left unopened...

CONTENTS

Chapter 1

THE LITTLE DOOR

Two girls walk along a **DARK** pavement.

Tree branches block the moonlight.

It is late.

The girls, Anna and Rose, are **leaving** a friend's birthday party. They each carry a box filled with leftover cake.

"Race you home!" Anna shouts. She laughs and quickly runs away.

Rose doesn't run after her friend.

She knows Anna is faster.

Rose sighs. She keeps walking.

Anna keeps running. She turns a corner.

Up ahead, a **SHADOW** stands next to the pavement. Anna stops a metre or so back.

A tiny wooden box sits on top of a wooden post. It looks like a bird house.

Anna steps **closer**. *Is this a free library?* she wonders. *Brilliant! I love books.*

Anna reaches towards the library's small door.She lifts a rusty hook and unlocks it.

CREAK! The wooden door swings open.

Anna reaches in.

A scaly claw reaches out.

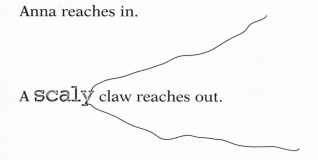

Chapter 2

DON'T OPEN IT!

Rose hears a **terrifying** scream.

She calls out, "Anna! Where are you?"

Rose runs down the pavement. She turns the corner.

Something white is on the pavement.
Rose picks it up.

It is Anna's cake box.

CREAK! A small lending library sits on a post about a metre away.

Rose hadn't noticed it before.

The little house is **rocking** in the wind.
Every time it rocks, it creaks.

Rose knows how much Anna likes books.

Rose walks over to the small wooden house.

She looks closer.

Cake icing is **smeared** on the edge of the door.

Rose carefully lifts the rusty hook.

The door opens with a **BANG!**

A scaly claw grabs Rose's arm.

Before she can scream, the claw pulls her inside.

Then the door slams shut.

The wooden post rocks back and forth.

POP! The post pushes itself up from the ground.

Two huge, scaly feet **sprout** from the post.

They look like the feet of a giant crow. The wrinkled claws scrape the pavement.

Two white boxes rest on the concrete.

The feet **squash** them as the lending library scurries away.

Chapter 3

PRISONERS OF THE NEST

Rose opens her eyes. She screams.

She is standing in a giant bird's nest.

The nest is made from **ripped** book covers and torn pages.

Twelve **ENORMOUS** eggs rest in the middle.

One of the eggs rocks back and forth.

Rose steps closer.

She hears a girl's voice. It is Anna's voice.

It is coming from **inside** the egg.

"Hey!" someone whispers.

Rose turns around.

A boy is peeking out from behind a pile of old books.

"Over here!" he says.

There are others hiding with the boy.

"I have to help my friend," says Rose.

"You shouldn't have **SCREAMED**," says the boy. "Now the bird monster will swallow you."

"Monster?" Rose says, trembling. "Monsters only exist in fairy tales."

A dark-haired girl stares at her.

"Then how did your friend get inside that egg?" she asks.

CREAK! CREAK!

A loud screeching sound fills the air.

They cover their ears.

A vast **shadow** appears over them.

A monstrous bird flaps above them.

Its wings are dark and dirty.

Its feathers are made of shredded book covers and **sharp** hooks.

Its eyes are the colour of rust.

The bird turns one eye towards Rose. It screams.

Chapter 4

OPEN IT!

"Get away!" shouts Rose. "Get away!"

The giant bird lunges at Rose with its beak. She **SCREAMS** and takes a step back.

The dark-haired girl catches Rose before she falls.

The two girls hold each other. They lean against an old book and catch their breath.

The **tattered** cover of the old book begins to glow.

Rose reads the title. **ROSE RED AND SNOW WHITE**. It is her favourite fairy tale.

She sees the other girl's hand is still on the book, too.

An idea hatches in Rose's brain. "What is your name?" Rose asks.

"Blanche," says the dark-haired girl. "It means **White**."

"I knew it!" says Rose.

She opens the book. The pages glow even brighter. Then the light takes the shape of a young man in red.

Chapter 5

DEFEATING EVIL

"Get down," the man in red says.

He aims a glowing red hand at the bird flapping above them.

The creature screams. Wings **shatter**.

Pages rain **down** on the nest. It bursts into a ball of light.

Crack! The eggs hatch. People climb out of the broken shells. Rose runs to hug Anna.

Rose turns to the man in red. "Who are you?" she asks.

"The Red Librarian," the man says. "I've been hunting that Digest Bird for years. It escaped from the Library of Doom long ago."

"But how did you get here?" asks Rose.

"You and your new friend shared the right book at the right time," says the Red Librarian. "Sometimes that's all it takes to destroy evil."

A gust of wind **chills** them to their bones. They close their eyes.

When they open their eyes, they are back on the pavement.

The free library has **GONE**.

On the cement are two new white boxes. Inside each box is a fresh slice of cake.

GLOSSARY

bloodshot if someone's eyes are bloodshot, their eyes have many red lines caused by a lack of sleep, illness or stress.

devour quickly eat all of something in a way that shows that you are very hungry

digest biological process of changing food that you have eaten into simpler forms that can be used by the body. Digest can also refer to a magazine or collection of written material.

lunge sudden forward or downward movement done in a forceful or aggressive way

monstrous extremely large, vicious mean, beastly or violent

shattered if you have shattered something, you have destroyed it by breaking it into many pieces

tattered old, torn, worn or falling apart

DISCUSSION QUESTIONS

1. Have you ever seen a small lending library? Would you borrow any books from one? Why or why not?

2. The Red Librarian wears a uniform of leather. As he works with books, why do you think he has a uniform like this?

3. Why do you think the giant bird was trapping young people in the libraries? What did it want?

WRITING PROMPTS

1. When Rose and the dark-haired girl touched the same book, the Red Librarian was summoned. What do you think the title of that book was? Make your own title and write a short description of what you think the book was about.

2. The Red Librarian calls the monstrous bird in this story a "Digest". Read the two meanings of the word "digest" in the glossary on the previous page. Write about why it's a good or bad name for the creature, and why.

3. The hero in this book is the Red Librarian. He has some special abilities and powers. Make a list of the ones he uses in this story. Then write about which one you would like to have for yourself.

THE AUTHOR

Michael Dahl is the prolific author of the bestselling *Goodnight, Baseball* picture book and more than 200 other books for children and young adults. He has won the AEP Distinguished Achievement Award three times for his non-fiction, a Teachers' Choice Award from *Learning* magazine and a Seal of Excellence from the Creative Child Awards. He is also the author of the Hocus Pocus Hotel mystery series and the Dragonblood books. Dahl currently lives in Minnesota, USA.

THE ILLUSTRATOR

Bradford Kendall has enjoyed drawing for as long as he can remember. As a boy, he loved to read comic books and watch old monster films. He graduated from the Rhode Island School of Design with a BFA in Illustration. He has owned his own commercial art business since 1983. Bradford lives in Rhode Island, USA, with his wife, Leigh, and their two children, Lily and Stephen.